I Am Ace the Great:

a story about sports

by Jasmine Furr

Illustrated by Ashleigh Sharmaine & Designed by Adam Hopkins

ISBN 978-1-7331667-2-0
Library of Congress Control Number: 2019912225

Untraditional Publishing Company, LLC
St. Louis, MO
orders@theachieversbooks.com

Every day when Ace wakes up,
he sees his parents and, with so much love,
they give him a list of sentences to say
to prepare him for an amazing day:
"I am smart!”
“I am brave!”
“I am happy!”
“I am great!”
"I am Ace the Great and today is my day!"

"I am smart"
"I am brave"
"I am happy"
"I am great"
A
Ace

So, Ace went to class to lead the greeting.
His classmates chose
how they said, "good morning."
They could hug, shake hands, or fist bump.
Ace greeted each student, one by one.
He said, "Thank you for saying
'good morning' to me!"
Ace said, "I am happy!"

1
Ace

At lunchtime, Ace took a first look
at his brand new picture book.
He flipped the pages and read to his friends
King, Queen, and Allison.
Ace read loud enough for everyone to hear.
His friends laughed and cheered.
The ending was everyone's favorite part.
"Thank you," Ace said, "I am smart."

Ace

It was dodgeball day during recess.
Ace was the captain because he was the best.
He could pick anyone to be on his team.
Playing dodgeball was Kate's dream,
but Duke said that Kate was the worst.
"That's not nice." Ace said, "I will pick her first."

Ace

Kate did great without a doubt.
She threw the ball at Duke
and screamed "you're out!"
Ace and Kate had a great game.
Ace said, "I am brave!"

After dodgeball, Ace went to class.
Learning about science was a blast.
He made a volcano that stood 2 feet tall
with lava pouring over it all.
It was fun to see. Ace did his part.
"I did it." Ace said, "I am smart."

1
Ace

After school, Ace had dinner with his football team.
Winning the game was their dream.
He told them, "I believe in you and me."
Ace said, "I am happy."

Ace and his team walked on the field.
He ran with the ball with his hand as a shield.
His family could see him, and they looked proud.
Then everyone screamed, "Touchdown!"
Ace and his team won the game.
"Awesome!" Ace said, "I am brave."

1

Ace's friends and family came over to him
to celebrate an amazing win.
Ace said, "All of the sentences came true."
"Great!" they said, "What did you do?"
Ace replied,
"I went to school, and I greeted my class.
I read out loud and made everyone laugh.
My friend and I played dodgeball.
Then I made a volcano that was tall.
I had dinner with my football team
and we won the game for all to see."

"My entire day was as great as me!
Can you believe all that I achieved?
In just one day, I can say:
'I am smart!'
'I am brave!'
'I am happy!'
'I am great!'
I did all of this because I believed!
I did all of this because I am me!"

TM

CPSIA information can be obtained
at www.ICGtesting.com
Printed in the USA
BVHW061921231120
593975BV00001B/1

9781733166720